NIGHT NOISES

Written by

Lisa Beere

Illustrated by

Lynn Costelloe

Edited by

Veronica Castle

Published by

Crimson Cloak Publishing

All Rights Reserved

ISBN 13: 978-1-68160-200-4

ISBN 10: 1-68160-200-8

Publisher's Publication in Data

Beere, Lisa

Night Noises

   1. Illustrated 2. Color 3. Juvenile Fiction 4. Kindness and Consideration 5. Family 6. Night Fears

It was time for me to go to bed. I went to my room and I put on my *special* pajamas. They are my favorite because they have puppies on them.

After that I went to the bathroom and brushed my teeth. I even combed *all* of the hair on my head.

Then it was time for hugs and kisses. So I went to the living room and loudly announced to everyone "I am ready."

First, I gave a goodnight kiss to Grandpa and then one to Nan.

Then, my Dad wanted a *really* big hug!

Next, I had a hug and a kiss from Mom, and a handshake from my older sister Junie.

After all that, Mom took my hand and together we walked to my room. She lifted up my blankets and I crawled into my bed.

"Goodnight Sam," Mom said. And she gave me one last kiss. Then Mom turned out my lights and said, "Goodnight," again.

Now, I am in my room all alone and it is dark. I close my eyes and try to sleep.

Cheep! Cheep! Cheep!

Aaaah!!! *What is that*?!

I yell loudly for Mom.

She comes running into my room. And *all* the lights go back on.

"What's wrong?" Mom asks.

"I can't sleep! I tried, but I heard something say: ***Cheep! Cheep! Cheep!***"

Mom smiles and says, "No problem." She leans over me and closes my window. "How is it now?" she asks.

"Thank you Mom; *now* I can sleep."

Then Mom turns out my lights again and says "Goodnight."

I close my eyes and *try* to sleep.

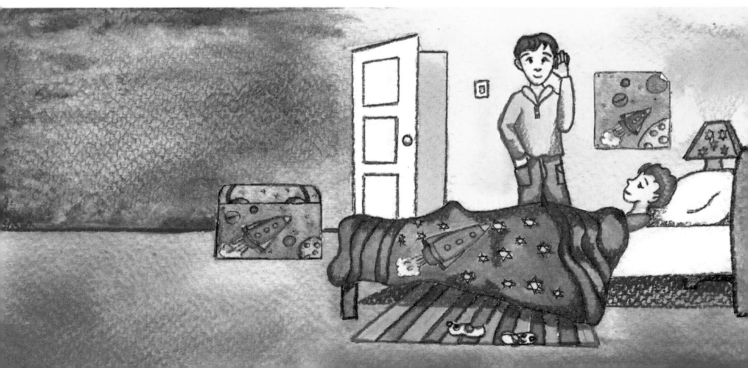

BAM! BAM! BAM!

Aaaah!!! *What is that*?!

I yell for my Dad.

Dad comes running into my room.

And *all* the lights go back on.

"What's wrong?" Dad asks.

"I can't sleep! I tried, but I heard something go: *BAM! BAM! BAM!"*

Dad smiles and says, "I'll take care of it."

Then he yells at my sister Junie to turn off her music.

Suddenly, there is silence from the next room.

"How is it now?" Dad asks.

"Thank you Dad, *now* I can sleep."

Then Dad turns out my lights and says, "Goodnight."

I close my eyes and *try* to sleep.

Thump! Thump! Thump!

Aaaah!!! *What is that*?!

I yell for Grandpa.

He comes running into my room.

And *all* the lights go back on.

"What's wrong?" Grandpa asks, looking quite worried.

"I can't sleep! I *tried* Grandpa, but I heard something make a *Thump! Thump! Thump!*"

Grandpa smiles and thinks.
Then he says, "Wait here a minute." And he leaves my room.

From outside I hear: **Snap! Snap! Snap**!

Aaaah!!! *What is that*?!

I yell for Grandpa.

He comes running, back into my room.

"What's wrong?" he asks.

"I heard something outside go **Snap! Snap! Snap!**"

Grandpa smiles, "that was *just me* outside. I was cutting the tree branches that were hitting the house. They were making the *thump, thump, thump* that you heard. Now that I have cut the branches, it should be much quieter."

"Thank you Grandpa, *now* I can go to sleep."

Then Grandpa turns out my lights and says "Goodnight."

I close my eyes and *try* to sleep.

Tick. Tick. Tick.

Aaaah!!! *What is that*?!

This time, I yell for Nan.

She comes running into my room.

And *all* the lights go back on.

"What's wrong?" Nan asks. She looks a bit tired.

"I can't sleep! I *tried* Nan, but I heard a sound. It was a ***tick, tick, tick****!"*

Nan sighs and says, "It's your clock making that sound, Sam. Don't worry, I will take it with me and keep it in the kitchen where you can't hear it. It won't bother you any more."

"Thank you Nan, *now* I can go to sleep."

Then Nan turns out my lights and says "Goodnight."

I close my eyes and *try* to sleep.

Silence.

There is *no* noise.

It is so quiet.

It is *too* quiet!

I hear nothing.

Not a *thump*.

Not a *snap*.

No *bam*.

Not even a little *cheep*.

Aaaah!!! I can't sleep!

I yell as loud as I can!

"AAAAH!"

Nan comes running as fast as she can into my room.

"What's wrong?" she asks. And *all* the lights go back on.

Dad and Mom come running into my room too.

"What's wrong?" They both ask.

Then Grandpa *also* comes into my room.

"What's going on?" he says.

I am not sure what to say.

I feel a little bit silly for *still* being scared.

Junie comes into my room then too.

I tell my family, "I can't sleep. I *did* try."

They all look at each other.

I can tell Nan is thinking for a moment. Then she has an idea.

"Sam," she asks, "Are you worried about being alone?"

"Maybe," I answer.

"Sam, you know Junie sleeps in the next room," says Mom.

"I know."

"And Mom and I are *just* down the hallway," says Dad. "We will all hear you if you call us."

"And Nan and I are just downstairs," adds Grandpa. "You can always come and get us."

"We are *all here* if you need us," says Mom. "And now *we need* you to go to sleep, it's getting quite late."

"But there is no one *in here* with me!" I say.

I didn't see Junie disappear.

She came back, running into my room.

"HERE!" she says and hands me her favorite Teddy Bear. "Now you are not alone. *Teddy* will be with you."

That was *actually* really nice of her.

"Thank you," I say, taking the bear. "*Now* I can go to sleep."

Thank you for taking the time to read this book. If you enjoyed it, please consider telling your friends or posting a short review. Word of mouth is an author's best friend and much appreciated.

About the Author

Lisa Beere is an Ottawa writer creating in the areas of poetry, short stories, children's literature and romance. Her poetry has appeared in Ottawa Poetry Magazine and Meat for Tea: The Valley Review. Her first screenplay became the film Cindy's Gauntlet (2015). Her book Equal to The Challenge: An Anthology of Women's WWII Stories was published in 2001 under the name Banister. She loves family time, fine dining, theatre, white water rafting and singing.

https://www.facebook.com/SparkleAuthor/
https://ca.linkedin.com/in/lisa-beere-5888a118
http://www.canscaip.org/Sys/PublicProfile/29992144
https://www.scbwi.org/members-public/lisa-beere

Find news about new books by Lisa Beere at:

http://lisa.beere.ca

http://main.crimsoncloakpublishing.com/lisa-beere.html

CPSIA information can be obtained
at www.ICGtesting.com
Printed in the USA
BVOW10s2005081116

467001BV00003B/5/P